PRINCESS PENELOPE TAKES CHARGE!

by Todd Mack ♛ illustrated by Julia Gran

scholastic inc.

new york toronto london auckland sydney
mexico city new delhi hong kong buenos aires

For John,
my big little prince
– T.M.

To Rebecca and Aaron,
Zoe and Ian
– J.G.

PENELOPE was a princess.
She had absolutely everything.

Her room was filled with books
and toys, crayons and clothes.
She had dolls to play with
and stuffed animals to cuddle.
But there was one thing Penelope
was missing. More than anything,
she wanted to be
A BiG SiSTER.

So when her mommy and daddy told her that

they were going to have a baby,

Penelope cheered,

"I'M PENELOPE, AND I'M GOING TO BE A BIG SISTER!"

Penelope watched as her
mommy's tummy grew
bigger and bigger
and rounder
and rounder.

We're having a baby

Penelope told everyone that HER tummy was growing bigger and bigger and rounder and rounder because SHE was going to have a baby, too.

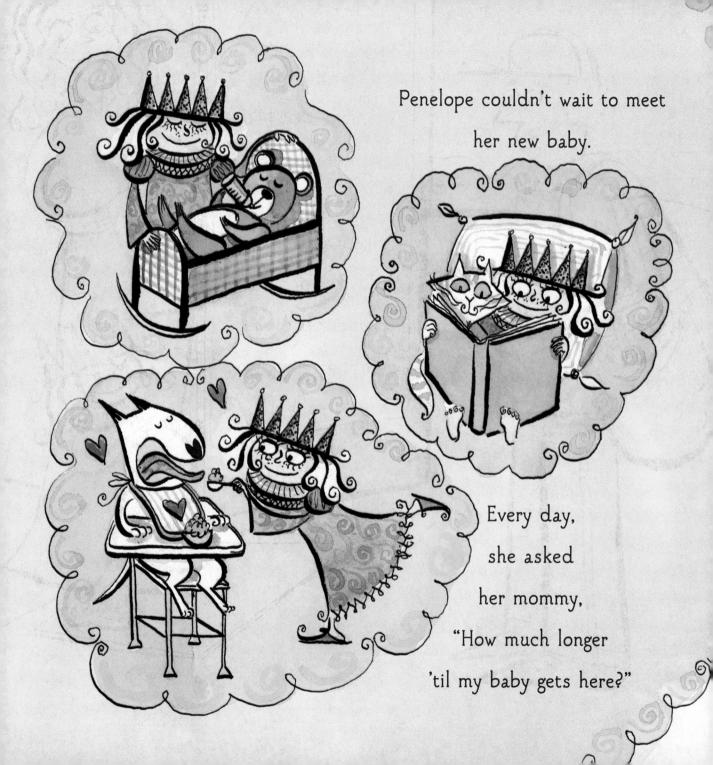

Penelope couldn't wait to meet her new baby.

Every day, she asked her mommy, "How much longer 'til my baby gets here?"

"Just be patient
a little bit longer," her mommy said,
"until after Valentine's Day."

Every night,
Penelope dreamed
about her baby.

After Valentine's Day, Penelope's

favorite auntie came to visit.

She brought her a new doll and a pink T-shirt.

Penelope named her doll MARIGOLD,

and dressed her in her favorite dress.

WEL COME HO

That day, Penelope's parents went to the hospital to have the baby.

"Do you think you're going to have a baby brother or a baby

sister?" Penelope's auntie asked.

"I already know it's going to be a girl," Penelope replied
matter-of-factly. She raised her glass and cheered,
"TO MY NEW BABY SISTER!"

The next morning,
Penelope's daddy
came home
and announced,
"Penelope, you have
a new baby brother!
His name is
DEXTER."

"A BROTHER?!"

Penelope shrieked.

"I don't want a baby brother!
Go back and
trade him in for a girl."

Penelope ran to her room.
A baby brother was NO fun.
You couldn't play dress up and
tea party and princess with a BOY.

All that day, Penelope moped around the house.

She wouldn't even play with her auntie.

"I don't want a baby brother," she complained to Marigold.
"I ONLY WANT A BABY SISTER, JUST LIKE YOU."

The next day,
Mommy and
Dexter came home.
"Say hello
to your new
BABY
BROTHER,"
said Mommy.

Penelope's stomach felt a little squooshy.

"Hi, Dexter," she said.

"I'm Penelope, and I'm your big sister, but you can't play with me because you're just a silly ol' boy. You don't even have any hair."

Mommy gave Penelope a big hug.

"You'll see," she said.

"He'll be lots of fun."

BUT
PENELOPE
DIDN'T
BELIEVE
HER.

Penelope watched as her mommy
cradled Dexter in her arms.

Penelope cradled Marigold in her arms.
"OH, MARIGOLD," she said. "YOU'RE SOOO CUTE.
I LOVE YOU MORE THAN ANYTHING."

Mommy was wrong about Dexter. He was no fun.

On Mother's Day,
Penelope and Marigold
dressed up in
their fanciest clothes.
But Dexter wore a boring onesie,
just like he always did.

On the Fourth of July,
Penelope and Marigold sang and
danced all day long. But Dexter
lay there sleeping, just like
he always did.

And when all the leaves fell down in autumn, Penelope and
Marigold put on their favorite sweaters and built a huge leaf pile to
jump in. But Dexter only watched, just like he always did.

Then, one day, Penelope noticed something.
DEXTER HAD HAIR,
and it was the same color as hers.

"Can I brush Dexter's hair and put bows and ribbons in it?"
Penelope asked her mommy.

Soon, Penelope started to help her mommy and daddy take care of Dexter.

IT WAS A BIG JOB.

Sometimes, Penelope's
mommy and daddy
needed coaching.

"NO, DAD,
THIS IS HOW
YOU DO IT,"
Penelope instructed.

"Penelope,
WE DON'T KNOW WHAT WE WOULD DO WITHOUT YOU,"
her mommy and daddy often said.

After a while,
Penelope decided that maybe
Dexter was FUN to play with—

even if Dexter didn't always
ENJOY playing with Penelope.

Every night, Penelope
helped put Dexter to bed.
She read him a book
and sang him her
favorite lullaby.
"I'M PENELOPE, AND I'M
YOUR BIG SISTER."

Penelope was a princess.
She had absolutely
everything.